K-2   J 20831
Kin   Kinnell, Galway
            How the alligator
        missed breakfast

ORANGE CITY PUBLIC LIBRARY
Orange City, Ia.

1. Items are returnable on the latest date stamped
   on the due date card in this pocket. Items may
   be renewed once except books on reserve.
2. Magazines may be kept one week and may be
   renewed once for the same period.
3. A fine of five cents a day will be charged on
   each item which is not returned on its due date.
4. All injuries to any library materials beyond
   reasonable wear, and all losses shall be made
   good to the satisfaction of the Librarian.

DEMCO

How the Alligator Missed Breakfast

GALWAY KINNELL

Illustrated by Lynn Munsinger

Houghton Mifflin Company   Boston   1982

J 20831

Library of Congress Cataloging in Publication Data
Kinnell, Galway, 1927-
How the alligator missed breakfast.

Summary: Elp the Alligator has so many adventures
one morning that he can't manage to eat breakfast.
[1. Alligators—Fiction. 2. Animals—Fiction]
I. Munsinger, Lynn, ill. II. Title.
PZ7.K622Ho   [E]   82-3029
ISBN 0-395-32436-X   AACR2

Copyright © 1982 by Galway Kinnell
Copyright © 1982 by Lynn Munsinger

All rights reserved. No part of this work may be
reproduced or transmitted in any form or by any means,
electronic or mechanical, including photocopying and
recording, or by any information storage or retrieval
system, except as may be expressly permitted by the 1976
Copyright Act or in writing by the publisher. Requests
for permission should be addressed in writing to Houghton
Mifflin Company, 2 Park St., Boston, Massachusetts 02108.

Printed in the United States of America

H 10 9 8 7 6 5 4 3 2 1

Miss Hiphop Becomes Interested in Flying

On this particular morning, Arnold the Crow was flying above the trees and thinking about breakfast. When the trees were tall, he flew up. When they were short, he flew down.

Suddenly he heard a strange cry: "Hey-elp!"

He coasted and listened. There it was again: "Hey-elp!"

Arnold flew down and found a rabbit sitting on a rock in the middle of a pond.

"Hello," he said. "I'm Arnold. Who are you?"

"I'm Miss Hiphop," said the rabbit.

"Who's this Elp you're calling for?"

"Elp?" said Miss Hiphop. "I don't know anyone named

Elp. It's just that I want to get home and have breakfast, but I can't get off this rock. You see, I don't know how to swim. I was hoping somebody would come along and give me some hey-elp."

"Oh," said Arnold. He thought for a few moments. "Well," he said, "if you don't know how to swim, why don't you fly?"

"Fly? Rabbits can't fly, you silly crow."

"Of course they can. Anyone can fly. Here, I'll teach you."

Arnold showed Miss Hiphop how to flap her ears as if they were wings. She practiced awhile.

"Are you ready?" said the crow.

"I think so," said Miss Hiphop.

"Before you fly away," said Arnold the Crow, "I have a question. If you didn't fly, how did you manage to get onto this rock in the middle of the pond in the first place?"

"Now that you mention it, how did I?" Miss Hiphop said. "All I know is, I was sitting on a rock by the edge of the pond, and in no time at all I found I was out here in the middle, sitting on the same rock. Do you think the rock moved?"

"Hmmmm," said Arnold, not believing a word of it. "I doubt it. Well, now. Are you ready to fly? Then get set. Go!"

Miss Hiphop took a great hiphop into the air and flapped her ears as fast as she could.

The sun was just coming up, and it would have been a very pretty morning for Miss Hiphop to fly into if she had been able to. Unfortunately, she at once fell back onto the rock.

Well, not exactly a rock. For just at that moment Elp the Alligator woke up and opened his eyes.

"Well," he said, looking cross-eyed at the rabbit perched on his forehead. "I *thought* I heard someone calling me."

Elp the Alligator ferried Miss Hiphop to shore, and then she invited him and Arnold to come to her house for breakfast. They both accepted. Miss Hiphop told them where she lived and hiphopped away home. The crow followed her over the tree tops. Elp the Alligator set off on foot along the road.

A Ride in a Bathtub
and Elp's New Automobile

Elp the Alligator did not like walking on land. The pebbles hurt his feet, for one thing. For another, he liked swimming better. Best of all, he liked riding on logs. So when a bathtub came strolling past, looking for children with dirt and grease all over them from rolling down hills, Elp the Alligator climbed aboard.

His head stuck out in front, and his tail stuck out behind. It was a very comfortable way to travel.

The bathtub stopped whenever it saw a dirty child.

"Would you like a bath?" it asked.

"No, thank you," each child answered politely. The reason was that they saw there was an alligator in the bathtub already.

After a while, Elp and the bathtub came to an automobile parked at the edge of a swamp. Elp climbed out of the bathtub and went over to it. He did not own an automobile because alligators never own automobiles, but he liked them all the same. He liked the firm way they said "Beep! Beep!" whenever they found somebody in their path.

Pinned on the automobile was a note:

I THREW AWAY THIS AUTOMOBILE.
WHOEVER FINDS IT MAY KEEP IT.
SIGNED: A TOAD

"Fine," thought Elp. "I am the one who found it, so I shall keep it."

Elp lived on the other side of the swamp, and he wondered how he would get his new automobile home. Whether he swam home or walked home, he wouldn't be able to carry it in his arms. Nor did he have any way to tie the automobile to his back. The only place alligators have room for luggage is inside their tails. But because there is no zipper on their tails, they have to swallow whatever it is they want to put into their tails. So Elp swallowed the automobile and gulped a few times to get it positioned well back in his tail. But when he started to

swim home, the automobile made him so tail-heavy that
he sank at once. Only his head stuck up out of the water.
"Hey-elp!" cried Elp.

Pretty soon, Arnold the Crow came flying along. He had been sent back by Miss Hiphop to find out why Elp had not appeared for breakfast. When he saw Elp he called out to him, "Hey, Elp!"

Elp looked up and saw the crow. "What's wrong?" he said. "You in trouble?"

"Oh, no," said Arnold. "All's well. Except that you and I are about to have breakfast with Miss Hiphop and here you are, having yourself a nice soak in the swamp."

"Well, if I were you, I wouldn't fly around crying for hey-elp, when all is well," said Elp. "Someday when you do need hey-elp, no one will listen."

"Hey, Elp, do hurry up!" said Arnold. "I'm hungry."

"There, you're doing it again!" said Elp. "Anyway, I can't hurry because there is an automobile in my tail. It's weighing me down so I can't swim. Can you give me a little hey-elp?"

"I have an idea," said Arnold. "Why don't you take the automobile out of your tail and then *drive* it home?"

"That might be a good idea," said Elp. "Hmmm. Possibly a very good idea."

He took the automobile out of his tail and got into the driver's seat.

"Tell Miss Hiphop I have to take my new automobile home, so I won't be able to make it for breakfast," said Elp. "But thank her anyway and tell her I'll try to get there in time for lunch," he shouted back as he drove away.

Elp drove along the edge of the swamp as fast as his

new car would go. Whenever there was anybody in his way, he went "Beep, Beep!" making them jump.

"How clever Elp is," all the other alligators remarked to each other as he drove by. "*We* probably would have tried to take the automobile home in our tails."

Miss Hiphop Flies

That same morning Mr. Prickle the Porcupine decided he would get a haircut before going to his usual restaurant for breakfast. The reason was that the last time he went to the restaurant for breakfast he accidentally prickle-prackled several customers as he squeezed past their tables.

The barber had never cut a porcupine's hair before, and naturally he made a few mistakes. Using electric hedge clippers, he cut Mr. Prickle's back too flat and left all the quills at the tail sticking up. As a result, Mr. Prickle looked very much like a chair when he came out of the barbershop.

At the restaurant, they wouldn't let Mr. Prickle in.

"We don't serve breakfast to chairs, even if they *are* hungry," the waiter said, after Mr. Prickle had protested a few times. "We sit on them, and we have quite enough chairs already."

Mr. Prickle huddled outside the restaurant, feeling very mad at his barber for making him look like a chair. Just then, along came Miss Hiphop. She was carrying a notebook. She had finished eating breakfast with Arnold the Crow and now she was looking for a nice place to sit and write down some ideas on the subject of how rabbits can learn to fly. Seeing what she thought was a chair, she sat down on it.

"Yipes!" she cried. She was very prickle-prackled on the bottom and, flapping her ears, flew high into the air.

Mr. Prickle expected that when Miss Hiphop came back down she would be angry with him for pretending to be a chair. Instead, when Miss Hiphop landed, she looked blissful.

"So *that's* what it's like to fly!" she said, and started scribbling in her notebook.

Mr. Prickle Prickle-Prackles Again

Back at the barbershop, Mr. Prickle complained to the barber about his chairlike haircut.

"We'll fix that," said the barber. "Don't worry! You see, you were my first porcupine. It takes a little practice. This time I'll get it right."

He took out his electric hedge clippers and went to work on Mr. Prickle's quills all over again.

When he finished, the barber stood back and asked the

others waiting for haircuts if anyone thought Mr. Prickle still looked like a chair.

"No, he doesn't look in the least like a chair," they all agreed. "A little like a shoe, perhaps," one suggested, but Mr. Prickle had already left the shop and didn't hear.

Walking along the road, Mr. Prickle saw an automobile speeding toward him. He scrambled to the side of the road and crouched in the grass. Elp the Alligator was driving home in his new car.

"Well," Elp exclaimed, seeing Mr. Prickle crouching by the roadside. "What a lucky morning! Someone has thrown away a perfectly good shoe." He put on the brakes and got out of the car. "I've always hated walking on pebbly roads and hurting my feet. I'm the one who found the shoe, so I think I'll take it home." Suddenly he remembered Arnold the Crow's advice about getting the car home, and being an alligator who learns from experience, he decided he should *wear* the shoe and *walk* it home. And if he was going to walk it home, he realized at once, he would have to put the automobile back into his tail. So he swallowed the automobile once again and stepped into the shoe.

"Yipes!" he cried. His foot was so prickle-prackled he would have flown high into the air except that he couldn't because of the automobile in his tail.

"Hey-elp!" Elp cried.

"Stop talking to yourself, Elp," said Arnold the Crow, who just then happened to be flying by.

"I'm not talking to myself, I'm calling for hey-elp," said Elp. "I've stepped into this shoe and it is prickle-prackling my foot very badly."

"Elp," said Arnold, "that isn't a shoe, that's Mr. Prickle the Porcupine. The barber doesn't know how to cut a porcupine's quills and Mr. Prickle has come out looking like a shoe. That *is* you, isn't it, Mr. Prickle?"

"Yesssss," Mr. Prickle groaned, for he was all crushed under Elp the Alligator.

"Why don't you take your foot out of him and get back in your automobile and let poor Mr. Prickle go on his way?" Arnold said.

That is what Elp did.

Mr. Prickle was very mad at the barber for hair-cutting him into the shape of a shoe, and he went back to complain.

"Don't worry, we'll fix that in no time," said the barber, and once again he went at Mr. Prickle with his electric hedge clippers flashing.

A Narrow Escape

When Mr. Prickle, freshly barbered for the third time that morning, saw Elp's new automobile parked in the street, he knew he must be near Elp's place. He caught a faint whiff of something cooking. He had not yet had breakfast, so this seemed a particularly good time to go in and tell Elp he was sorry for prickle-prackling his foot. He knocked at the door.

"What luck!" exclaimed Elp, when he opened the door and saw Mr. Prickle on the doorstep. "Someone has left me a lovely big hat. He picked it up and was just about to stick it on his head when Mr. Prickle cried, "Stop! Stop! I'm not a hat! I'm Mr. Prickle! I've just had a new haircut!"

"Yipes!" cried Elp. "What a narrow escape! I was nearly prickle-prackled all over my head!"

"I just came by to apologize for prickle-prackling you on the foot," Mr. Prickle said. "But if I look like a hat now, I think I really need some hey-elp."

"What?"

"Hey-elp."

"Yes, I'm right here," said Elp. "What do you want?"

"Hey-elp."

"Yes, for heaven's sake, I'm here! Now what is it?"

"I need a place to hide until my quills grow back and I stop looking like chairs, shoes, and hats. I'm tired of prickle-prackling."

"Hmmmm … I've got it!" said Elp. "I've never seen anyone looking for a hat on a roof. I believe the safest place for you to wait for your quills to grow back is my roof."

J 20831

So Mr. Prickle climbed onto the roof and hoped that Elp was right.

Elp went back into his kitchen and broke two eggs into a frying pan. He had missed Miss Hiphop's breakfast and he was going to make up for it now with a delicious breakfast of fried eggs and toast. As he started to toast his toast, he thought of Mr. Prickle sitting up there on the roof maybe without having had any breakfast. He went out to offer him some fried eggs and toast.

He looked all over the roof but Mr. Prickle was nowhere
to be seen. The only thing he could see was a lovely big
hat.

"I'll just try it on," he said, "to see if it fits."

And he did.

"Yipes!" he cried.

"Oh, Elp. There I've gone and prickle-prackled you again," said Mr. Prickle, feeling very miserable.

"Never mind," said Elp, rubbing his prickle-prackled head. "Alligator heads aren't very easy to prickle-prackle anyway. Come inside. I've got some breakfast cooking."

Back in the kitchen, Elp looked into his frying pan.

"Where are my eggs?" he said. The eggs had disappeared.

Where *were* his eggs?

The Story of the Missing Eggs

As soon as Elp had gone outside to look for Mr. Prickle and ask him in for breakfast, one of the eggs, Boily McPoach by name, said to the other, Egbert Egglesworth, "Egbert, don't you find it hot in this frying pan?"

"Yes, I do," replied Egbert. "Very hot."

"And doesn't it seem to you it's getting hotter?" said Boily.

"It does," said Egbert. "Much hotter."

"Egbert, I think we are being fried," said Boily.

The two eggs leapt out of the frying pan, hopped to the windowsill, and jumped out the window. They ran and ran. They came to a cottage and, thinking it might be a good place to hide, jumped through an open window. They landed in a frying pan that, as luck would have it, was sizzling on the stove.

"Well, well. What a surprise!" said Mr. Likum Yokum, when he saw two eggs appear in his frying pan. "I was just remembering that I was out of eggs. Now I'll just get my toast and then I'll have a delicious breakfast."

When Mr. Likum Yokum turned to get his toast, the two eggs leapt out of the frying pan and jumped out of the window.

"Well, well," said Mr. Likum Yokum, when he returned with his toast. "I *knew* I was out of eggs."

"Whew!" said Boily McPoach.

"No more jumping through windows," said Egbert Egglesworth.

And the two eggs ran and ran, and were never heard from again.

A Scarecrow, A Scared Crow,
Miss Hiphop's Book, and The End

Feeling quite hungry by this time, Mr. Prickle went out into the corn field behind Elp's house and ate some corn for breakfast. It was very tasty. When he had finished, he noticed that the scarecrow standing nearby had lost its hat.

"Aha!" he said, as a thought came to him. He climbed up the scarecrow and placed himself on top of the scarecrow's head. The scarecrow immediately became a much scarier scarecrow with this large prickly hat on top of it.

"It will be nice to be a porcupine again once my quills

grow out," Mr. Prickle thought, "but in the meantime, this is a fine place to be a hat."

It turned out it was a very fine place indeed. The scarecrow was now so scary that not even the farmer dared to come into the field, and Mr. Prickle had the corn all to himself.

Arnold did come by for a mid-morning ear of corn, but he was so scared by the new scary scarecrow that he flew off, crying, "Hey-elp! Hey-elp!"

"Elp's not here," Mr. Prickle called after him, but Arnold did not hear.

As Arnold was getting over his fright, he spotted Elp riding in his old bathtub. Elp had forgotten all about his new automobile and had started out on foot looking for his missing eggs. After a while, when the bathtub came by, he remembered he liked riding better than walking and got in. Now he was having a good time speeding down hills in the bathtub, shouting "Beep! Beep!" at anyone who was in the way. He had also forgotten all about the eggs and breakfast.

"Hey, Elp!" called Arnold.

"What's wrong?" said Elp. "You in trouble again?"

"Forget it!" said Arnold, and he flew over to where

Miss Hiphop was writing the first chapter of her book, "Learning How to Fly, by a Rabbit."

"Here, let me hey-elp you," Arnold said. He faced Miss Hiphop and flapped his wings, and Miss Hiphop flapped her ears in reply. Elp, riding by in the bathtub, thought this was a very funny sight.

"Hey, Elp!" they both called out when they saw him, but Elp smiled a long alligator smile and rolled on by without a word.